Katy's First Haircut

Gibbs Davis

Illustrated by Linda Shute

HOUGHTON MIFFLIN COMPANY   BOSTON   1985

For Jory and Mara — G.D.

For Laurel — L.M.S.

Library of Congress Cataloging in Publication Data

Davis, Gibbs.
 Katy's first haircut.

 Summary: First-grader Katy begins to regret having
her long hair cut short after she is mistaken for a boy.
 1. Children's stories, American. [1. Haircutting—
Fiction. 2. School—Fiction] I. Shute, Linda, ill.
II. Title.
PZ7.D2886Kat   1985   [E]   85-2435
ISBN 0-395-38942-9

Text copyright © 1985 by Kathryn Kirby Gibbs Davis

Illustrations copyright © 1985 by Linda McElhiney Shute

Printed in the United States of America

Y 10 9 8 7 6 5 4 3 2 1

Katy had the longest hair of anyone in her class. It was so long she could tickle her cheek with it, tie it in a bow, even hide behind it. Katy loved her long hair. It made her feel special.

But lately her hair was becoming a lot of trouble.
Sometimes it got caught in her desk.

On windy days it blew in people's faces.

Katy's hair had gotten so long that when she did a
somersault she couldn't see which way was up and
which way was down.

Last week Tony and Fred decided to paint with Katy's braids instead of paintbrushes.

And this morning, when her mother tried to comb through the tangles little tears squeezed out of the corners of Katy's eyes.

"Stop!" shouted Katy. "Enough is enough!"

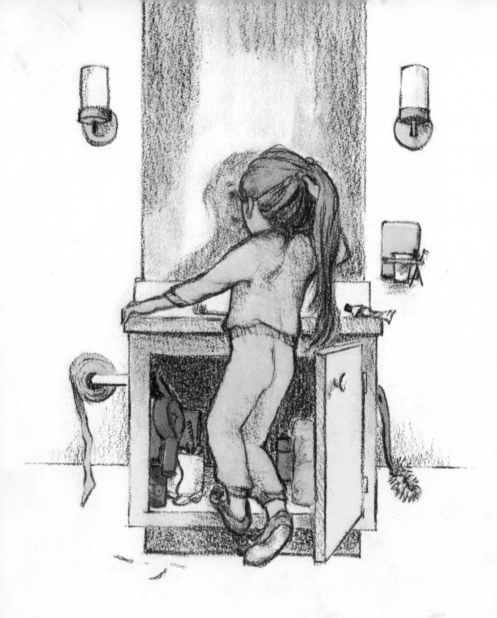

She thought about getting a haircut. But what would she look like with short hair? How would she feel?

Katy cut her doll's hair. Then she gave her bear a trim. They looked more grown-up. "I want to be grown-up, too," said Katy. Her mother and father had their hair cut once every month. "It's my turn now," she said.

"I want short hair," Katy told her parents.

"Your hair is beautiful," said her father. "Are you sure you want to have it cut?"

"It's my head!" said Katy. "And I want short hair!" She was absolutely certain.

"Okay," said Katy's mother. "Tomorrow we'll get our hair cut together. It'll be fun."

Katy was so excited about her first haircut she could hardly sleep that night. The next morning Katy put on her favorite shirt and went to the beauty salon with her mother.

Katy sat in the waiting room and watched customers come and go. They had curly hair, straight hair, brown, black, red, and yellow hair. Katy wondered what she'd look like when she left.

Katy felt important when the receptionist called her name.

Katy climbed up into a big chair next to her mother
and made faces in the mirror. She felt very grown-up.

First Katy's hair was washed. Then the hairdresser
got out a pair of scissors. It was fun watching her hair
get shorter and shorter. Katy closed her eyes and lis-
tened to the scissors "snip, snip." She almost fell
asleep while her hair was being dried.

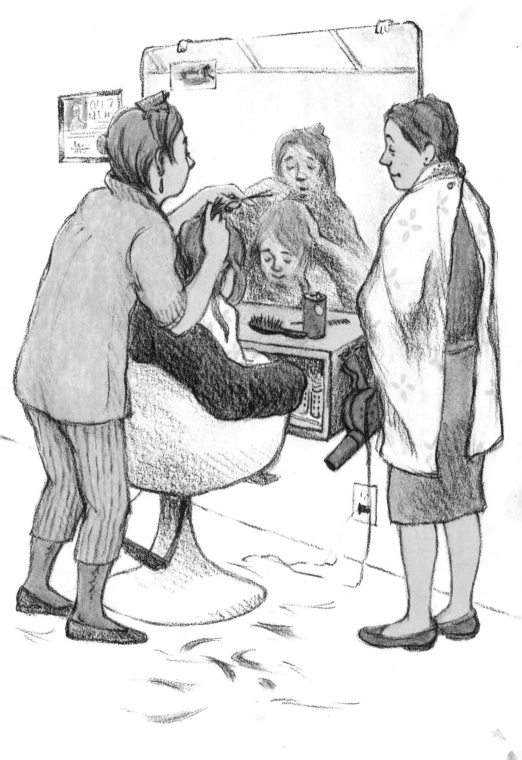

"All done," said the hairdresser. Katy opened
her eyes and looked at herself in the mirror. Katy
felt funny. She didn't look the same anymore. She
picked up some of her hair lying on the floor. She
felt like crying.

"Put it back!" she said.

"I can't," said the hairdresser. "You'll have to wait
for it to grow back."

"You look darling," said Katy's mother. "Let's buy
an ice cream cone to celebrate your first haircut."

Katy didn't feel like celebrating. Her beautiful long hair was gone. Even a double-dip ice cream cone didn't make her feel any better.

"What a cute little boy," said a woman in the store. She was looking straight at Katy.

"I'm a girl!" shouted Katy.

As soon as Katy got home she tried to tie a bow in her hair, but it was too short. She couldn't even tickle her cheek. It wouldn't reach.

"Your hair looks terrific," said Katy's father.

"I hate it," said Katy.

"Did you know you have a curl in the middle of your forehead now?" he said. But Katy was too sad to listen.

She went to bed early and dreamed of all the nice
things about long hair.

The next morning Katy raced to the mirror. Her hair was still short.

"You can take care of your own hair now," said Katy's mother.

It was easy combing short hair. There were no tangles so it didn't even hurt. But it was still short — too short.

Katy found a hat in the bottom of the hall closet and wore it to school.

"What a nice hat, Katy," said her teacher. "But why are you wearing it inside?"

"I have a cold," said Katy. She felt like hiding.

During art class, Fred bumped into Katy and her hat fell off. Before she could put it back on everyone had seen her short hair.

"Where's your hair?" asked Fred.

"I had it cut," said Katy.

Everyone was looking at her.

"But your hair was longer than anyone else's!" said Carol.

"Did your mom make you do it?" asked Tony.

"Of course not," said Katy. "I got my hair cut because I wanted to."

"What made you decide to cut your hair?" asked Katy's teacher.

Katy remembered all the terrible things about long hair. She remembered the time some girls tried to play tug-of-war with it. And when it got caught in her desk. But mostly she remembered crying every morning when her mother combed out the terrible tangles.

"Because enough is enough," said Katy. "Long hair is a lot of trouble."

"Good for you," said Katy's teacher. "It takes courage to make a big decision and go through with it. Let's all congratulate Katy for getting her first haircut."

Everyone cheered.

When Katy went out to recess, she felt the warm sun on her neck. She ran to the ladder and went down the slide. Waiting at the bottom was a girl with long hair.

"I'm getting my hair cut tomorrow," said the girl. "Is it scary?"

"Nope," said Katy. "You'll get used to it."

She did two somersaults in a row and her hair didn't get in her eyes once.